# From The Oak Tree

written by
## Tina Marie

illustrated by
## Steve Pileggi

Dedicated to my Mother who has passed, to her memory
and the portion of her that lives on in those she loved.
And to my Best Friend who has been both a mentor and
a constant inspiration by what she does, the character
she possesses and the life she lives.

"Aeker"   "Rhymes with Packer"

Spring has sprung in Cedar City, and a much too young squirrel has left his drey. Aeker has for the very first time opened his eyes and now made his way...

...oh dear, down I guess; into the laundry of one Mrs. Teeterbocker who seems to be missing for the moment and did not see the ungraceful, awkward descent of a tiny squirrel who now lay...

... in her fresh basket of linens with ribbons and lace. "What is this in my face?" A huge wet cold nose of a giant great dane. "Wait, wait" a strangely familiar tone calls out. "What is it that fell here to our house? Ooo... a baby squirrel, is he okay? I don't know. I'll take him to Mrs. Teeterbocker right away."

"Oh, what a sweet little thing, I'll call him Aeker and let him sleep with the pig." So Mrs. Teeterbocker placed Aeker gently in Lucy's bed and gave him some milk, some nuts and a pat on the head. "Good night little squirrel, lie down and sleep tight, by morning you'll feel just right."

So as Spring turned to Summer and Summer passed to Fall, Aeker grew stronger and quicker than them all. Of course it's not difficult to out run a pig, but Punk was a challenge when they raced to the twig.

In the midst of their games as they played and had fun,
in came two strangers quick, fast on the run. "Hey,
they ran up that tree," Aeker said to his friends.
"How did they do that, did anyone see?"

Amazed and bewildered by what he just saw,
he decided to follow and stretched out his paw.

Up ever slowly he climbed toward the top until he remembered and came to a stop. "Wait, I can't do this," he thought to himself, and then he cried out to Lucy for help.

Lucy ran to the tree, tried her hardest to climb, but slid down the trunk onto her behind. So Punk propped her up then stood nice and tall, they stretched out to Aeker and reached his rear paw.

Down came all three in a peculiar descent.
Aeker was safe now, thanks to his friends.

Lucy asked Aeker, "What happened up there?" Aeker said, "Lucy, I was so scared. I froze in my footsteps, my paws became numb. All I could think of is when I was young." So in for the nighttime went Aeker, Lucy and Punk to think of their day and be glad it was done.

As they rose the next morning and looked through the blinds, they saw Mrs. Teeterbocker seated by the pines. She's sipping her tea and having some bread before taking on what the day has ahead.

From The Oak Tree
By Tina Marie

So outside they ran to welcome the day, each one inventing a new game they could play. But Lucy was thinking, creating a plan. She hoped to see Aeker try climbing again.

Lucy asked Aeker, "So what would you think,
if Punk pulled the basket and stayed just beneath;
as you climbed the clothesline to try once again,
this time engaging the help of your friends?"

"Are you sure I can do this,
still think I should try?" "Yes,"
answered Lucy, "one paw at a time."

So out on the clothesline Aeker ventured to go...

"Hey Lucy, hey Lucy, look at me, look at me!
I'm climbing and crawling I can do it, can you see?"
"Yes, Aeker," Said Lucy. "I see you up there.
I knew you could do it, I'm so glad you're not scared!"

So as Fall turned to Winter and Winter passed to Spring,
Aeker learned that with good friends you can do anything.

"But there is a friend that sticks closer than a brother." Prov. 18:24